Monster Spray

For "Tails," who started the story,
and for E, who made the story come to life.

- Darrell

To my mom, for neverending encouragement,
and to DJ, my inspiration, my support, and
my humor twin.

- Esther

It wasn't the rickety washing machine clattering in the corner.

And it wasn't the mean looking furnace that scared her either.

No, Corey was scared of the monsters who lived in the basement.

They hid behind boxes, they hid behind shelves. They hid by throwing old blankets and sheets over themselves.

They hid in dark corners, they hid under the stairs. But Corey could always see their eyes, dozens of glowing pairs.

They wanted to scare her. They wanted her to scream. They wanted her to cry. They really were so mean!

She tried to tell her mom, she tried to tell her dad, but no one would believe her, which made Corey very sad.

Corey finally told her big sister, who came to her rescue. She gave Corey some advice, and told her exactly what to do.

"Now, Corey," her sister said, "want to get rid of the monsters? Here's an easy way: all we really need to do is make a batch of Monster Spray!"

First you take some water, then get some glitter, red and blue. Add a little lemon juice, and pinch of lavender too. Mix them all together, screw the cap on tight. Shake it up real well, and let it sit overnight.

The next day, Corey went back to the basement, armed with Monster Spray. She was still scared, but had to make the monsters go away...

She started down the stairs...
She could hear the monsters breath...
She knew that they were watching...
She got to the bottom step...

"No, please stop!" The monsters started to run.
They came out from their hiding spots;
no longer having fun.

"Please," they said, "please put away your spray. We didn't mean to scare you, we just thought you wanted to play!"

Corey looked at them and smiled, then put down her bottle of spray. "I like hide and seek. What do you like to play?"

We love hide and seek!

Now Corey and the monsters are friends, she goes to the basement every day. And together they play hide and seek, and she doesn't need her Monster Spray.

THE END

19681679R00015

Made in the USA
Middletown, DE
06 December 2018